The Keeping Quilt

SIMON & SCHUSTER BOOKS FOR YOUNG READERS
An imprint of Simon & Schuster Children's Publishing Division
1230 Avenue of the Americas, New York, New York 10020

SIMON & SCHUSTER BOOKS FOR YOUNG READERS is a trademark of Simon & Schuster, Inc.
For information about special discounts for bulk purchases, please contact
Simon & Schuster Special Sales at 1-866-506-1949 or business@simonandschuster.com.
The Simon & Schuster Speakers Bureau can bring authors to your live event. For more information or to book an event,
contact the Simon & Schuster Speakers Bureau at 1-866-248-3049 or visit our website at www.simonspeakers.com.
The text for this book is set in Lomba.
The illustrations for this book are rendered in two and six B pencils and acetone markers.
Manufactured in China · 0613 SCP
2 4 6 8 10 9 7 5 3 1
The Library of Congress has cataloged a previous edition as follows:
Polacco, Patricia. The keeping quilt / by Patricia Polacco.—Rev format ed.
p. cm. Summary: A homemade quilt ties together the lives of four generations of an immigrant Jewish family,
remaining a symbol of their enduring love and faith.
ISBN 978-0-689-82090-8 (hc)
[1. Quilts—Fiction. 2. Jews—Fiction. 3. Emigration and immigration—Fiction.] I. Title.
PZ7.P75186Ke · 1998 [E]—dc21 · 97-47690
ISBN 978-1-4424-8237-1 (25th-anniversary hc edition) · ISBN 978-1-4424-9070-3 (25th-anniversary eBook)

The Keeping Quilt

25TH ANNIVERSARY EDITION

PATRICIA POLACCO

SIMON & SCHUSTER BOOKS FOR YOUNG READERS

New York   London   Toronto   Sydney   New Delhi

The Keeping Quilt

When my Great-Gramma Anna came to America, she wore the same thick overcoat and big boots she had worn for farm work. But her family weren't dirt farmers anymore. In New York City, her father's work was hauling things on a wagon, and the rest of the family made artificial flowers all day.

Everyone was in a hurry, and it was so crowded, not like backhome Russia. But all the same it was their home, and most of their neighbors were just like them.

When Anna went to school, English sounded to her like pebbles dropping into shallow water. *Shhhhhh . . . Shhhhhh . . . Shhhhhh.* In six months she was speaking English. Her parents almost never learned, so she spoke English for them, too.

The only things she had left of backhome Russia were her
dress and babushka she liked to throw up into the air
when she was dancing.

And her dress was getting too small. After her mother had sewn her a new one, she took her old dress and babushka. Then from a basket of old clothes she took Uncle Vladimir's shirt, Aunt Havalah's nightdress, and an apron of Aunt Natasha's.

"We will make a quilt to help us always remember home," Anna's mother said. "It will be like having the family in backhome Russia dance around us at night."

And so it was. Anna's mother invited all the neighborhood ladies. They cut out animals and flowers from the scraps of clothing. Anna kept the needles threaded and handed them to the ladies as they needed them. The border of the quilt was made of Anna's babushka.

On Friday nights Anna's mother would say the prayers that started the Sabbath.
The family ate challah and chicken soup. The quilt was the tablecloth.

Anna grew up and fell in love with Great-Grandpa Sasha.
To show he wanted to be her husband, he gave
Anna a gold coin, a dried flower, and a piece of
rock salt all tied into a linen handkerchief.
The gold was for wealth, the flower
for love, and the salt so their
lives would have flavor.
   She accepted the hankie
and they were engaged.

Under the wedding huppa, Anna and Sasha promised each other love and understanding. After the wedding, the men and women celebrated separately.

When my Grandma Carle was born, Anna wrapped her daughter in the quilt to welcome her warmly into the world. Carle was given a gift of gold, flower, salt, and bread. Gold so she would never know poverty, a flower so she would always know love, salt so her life would always have flavor, and bread so that she would never know hunger.

Carle learned to keep the Sabbath and to cook
and clean and do washing.

"Married you'll be someday," Anna told Carle, and . . .

again the quilt became a wedding huppa, this time for Carle's wedding to Grandpa George. Men and women celebrated together, but they still did not dance together. In Carle's wedding bouquet were a gold coin, bread, and salt.

Carle and George moved to a farm in Michigan and
Great-Gramma Anna came to live with them. The quilt
once again wrapped a new little girl, Mary Ellen.

Mary Ellen called Anna, Lady Gramma. She had grown very old and was sick a lot of the time. The quilt kept her legs warm.

On Anna's ninety-eighth birthday, the cake was a kulich,
a rich cake with raisins and candied fruit in it.

When Great-Gramma
Anna died, prayers were
said to lift her soul to
heaven. My mother
Mary Ellen was now
grown up.

When Mary Ellen left home, she took the quilt with her.

When she became a bride, the quilt became her huppa. For the first time, friends who were not Jews came to the wedding. My mother wore a suit, but in her bouquet were gold, bread, and salt.

The quilt welcomed me, Patricia, into the world . . .

and it was the tablecloth for my first birthday party.

At night, I would trace my fingers around the edges of each animal on the quilt before I went to sleep. I told my mother stories about the animals on the quilt. She told me whose sleeve had made the horse, whose apron had made the chicken, whose dress had made the flowers, and whose babushka went around the edge of the quilt.

The quilt was a pretend cape when I was in the bullring,
or sometimes a tent in the steaming Amazon jungle.

At my wedding, men and women danced together. In my bouquet were gold, bread, and salt—and a sprinkle of wine, so I would always know laughter.

Many years ago I held Traci Denise
in the quilt for the first time.

Three years later my mother held
Steven John in the quilt for the
first time.

We were all so proud of Traci's
new baby brother.

Just like their mother, grandmother, and great-grandmother before them, they, too, used the quilt to celebrate birthdays and make superhero capes.

As the years passed and Traci and Steven were growing up,
their grandmother took pleasure at every family gathering
to tell the story of the quilt.

We all knew whose clothes made each flower and animal.

My mother was lucky enough to show the wonder
of this quilt to my brother's grandchildren,
her great-grandchildren.

When my mother died, prayers were said
to lift her soul to heaven. Traci and Steven
were now all grown up and getting ready to start
their own lives.

Now, as my children grow,
this quilt has become a part
of their hearts.

I decided to share its story with children everywhere, so I wrote a book to take with me on school visits for students to learn all about my family and traditions.

In time my son promised his life to his bride under this quilt.
I gave them both bread, so they would never know hunger;
salt, so that their lives would always have flavor; flowers, so
that they would know love; and, finally, a coin, so they would
never be poor of spirit.

When my daughter stood under this quilt to promise her heart to her partner, she too received bread, salt, flowers, and a coin.

As the years passed, the Keeping Quilt became fragile. Without my knowing, my son and daughter took digital photos of the quilt and sent them to my sister-in-law and her quilting guild.

The photos helped them make an exact pattern of the original. They even researched online to find the right fabrics to recreate the quilt. One heart from the original quilt was removed and added to the replica.

They talked about their own families
and traditions as they sewed.

My children presented the new quilt to me
as a complete surprise on my birthday.

Then I made a very hard decision.
With a bittersweet heart, I let the
original Keeping Quilt leave my care
to be on loan to the Mazza Museum
at the University of Findlay in
Findlay, Ohio.

It warms my heart to know that so many people will see the Keeping Quilt on display. Hopefully it will stir the beauty of memory and the richness of family in their souls and they will take these feelings away with them. They will create legacies of their own.

Now I take the new quilt to visit schools. Many hopeful brides and grooms have stood under it on their wedding day. It has covered many a table for special banquets. Children have run around, using it as a cape in the backyard. It has covered the coffins of those in our family whom we have loved and mourn. . . .

But best of all this quilt has
wrapped the most precious
gifts of all . . . new lives!

Dear ones,

For a quarter of a century now, this book has been a part of my life as well as yours.

It has been a heartfelt pleasure to chronicle the journey of this quilt from its creation at the turn of the century to present day.

It is gratifying that I have been able to witness personally the impact of this story on all of you. I am honored that you have given this book to loved ones to punctuate their own family milestones and, perhaps, to inspire new traditions.

Thank you all for being a part of this treasured celebration of kindred, family, and profound memory.

Patricia Polacco